FOLLOW CARL!

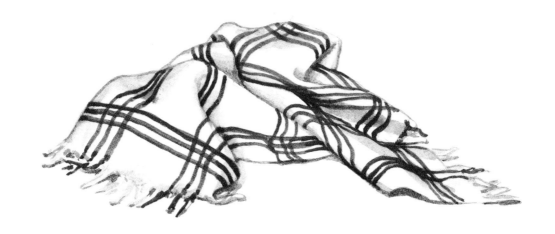

Follow Carl!

ALEXANDRA DAY

Farrar   Straus   Giroux

New York

By Alexandra Day

Carl Goes Shopping

Carl's Christmas

Carl's Afternoon in the Park

Carl's Masquerade

Carl Goes to Daycare

Carl Makes a Scrapbook

My Puppy's Record Book

Carl's Birthday

Carl's Baby Journal

By Christina Darling and Alexandra Day

Mirror

My heartfelt thanks to the children who accompanied Zabala (also known as Carl) on this adventure: Sophia Moran Schafer, Devin Thompson, Talia and Weylin Rose, James Ellis Rees, and Sally Slade

Library of Congress catalog card number: 97-76928
Distributed in Canada by Douglas & McIntyre Ltd.
Color separations by Prestige Graphics
Printed and bound in the United States of America by Berryville Graphics
First edition, 1998

The Carl character originally appeared in *Good Dog, Carl*
by Alexandra Day, published by Green Tiger Press

"Carl, can you come out and play Follow the Leader? You can be the leader!"